Care Bears™

The Day Nobody Shared

By Nancy Parent
Illustrated by Jay Johnson

ISBN 0-439-45157-4

CARE BEARS™ © 2003 Those Characters From Cleveland, Inc. Used under license by Scholastic Inc. All rights reserved. Published by Scholastic Inc.

SCHOLASTIC and associated logos are trademarks and/or registered trademarks of Scholastic Inc.

12 11 10 9 8 7 6 5 4 3 2 1   3 4 5 6 7 8/0

Printed in the U.S.A.

First printing, October 2003

SCHOLASTIC INC.
New York Toronto London Auckland Sydney
Mexico City New Delhi Hong Kong Buenos Aires

One day, Good Luck Bear got a box of rainbow bars in the mail.

He decided to hide the treats so he could have them all to himself.

"Hello," said Share Bear. "What are you doing?"

"I'm hiding my rainbow bars so I don't have to share them," Good Luck Bear whispered.

"But it feels so good to share," said Share Bear.
"It does?" asked Good Luck Bear.

"Come for a ride on the swings," said Share Bear.
"I'll tell you a story called The Day Nobody Shared."

Once upon a time, Cheer Bear made a giant ice-cream sundae with rainbow sprinkles that she wouldn't share with any of her friends.

Cheer Bear ended up with an awful tummy ache from eating the ice cream all by herself.

Then Bedtime Bear refused to share his special spot to watch the Care-a-lot parade.

But without Grumpy Bear to keep him awake,
Bedtime Bear fell asleep and missed the whole thing!

Hooray for Care Bears

WILDERMUTH

That afternoon, Tenderheart Bear wouldn't share his toys, so nobody wanted to play with him.

Tenderheart Bear quickly got bored. "Toys don't laugh and talk like friends," he said unhappily.

And when Love-a-lot Bear wouldn't share
her kite with Funshine Bear, he went
and played with Wish Bear instead.

"What bad luck that no one wanted to share,"
said Good Luck Bear.
"That's right," said Share Bear.

"If I share my rainbow bars," Good Luck Bear asked, "will that make everyone happy?"

"Yes," said Share Bear. "Sharing takes happiness and spreads it around. Sweetness goes a long way, if you're willing to share."

"I want to share these rainbow bars with our friends right now!" said Good Luck Bear.

"Great idea!" Share Bear replied.
"We can throw a sharing party in the park!"

When they passed Share Bear's house, Share Bear ran inside and came out with a bunch of balloons. "I'm going to share these!" said Share Bear.

"It feels really great to share," said Good Luck Bear.
"And it tastes yummy, too!" said Share Bear.